My Little Golden Book of
Cars and Trucks

By Chari Sue
Illustrated by Richard and Trish Courtney

A GOLDEN BOOK • NEW YORK

Western Publishing Company, Inc., Racine, Wisconsin 53404

Kenny loved playing with his car and truck collection more than anything in the world. He had a small model of practically every car and truck imaginable. His favorites were the race cars.

One day Kenny's father took him to the car and truck show in town. It was a very special day.

Kenny and his father drove to the show in their family car. It was a station wagon with plenty of room in the back for the dog and Kenny's toys when the family went on long trips. There was also a car seat for Kenny's younger sister.

Kenny saw lots of cars on the road. Some of them were like the one his family had, but some were small and sporty. Some were very old, and others were long and sleek. There were even cars without tops on them!

The car and truck show was in the county arena.
There was so much to see, Kenny didn't know
where to look first. "Let's start with cars and trucks
that are used in emergencies," said his father.

"Wow! Look at that fire engine," exclaimed Kenny as they began their tour. It was a big red truck that carried ladders and hoses to help fire fighters put out fires. Kenny was allowed to climb on board and wear the fire chief's hat.

Next was the ambulance. It had a loud siren to help it get through traffic in a hurry. "Many times a police car will go with the ambulance to the hospital," Kenny's father explained.

In the next area, Kenny saw cars and trucks that are used on farms. A man and a woman dressed in cowboy hats and boots explained how the different vehicles are used.

"The plow is used in the fields to turn up the soil. The combine harvester cuts, separates, and cleans the grain while moving over the field," said the woman.

"The forklift can be used to lift hay up to the barn," said the man. "And most farmers drive pickup trucks because they can carry grain, vegetables, and lots of other things."

"Can we go and look at those buses?" Kenny asked as he and his father walked on.

"Sure," his father answered. "That section has all the different vehicles that carry people from place to place."

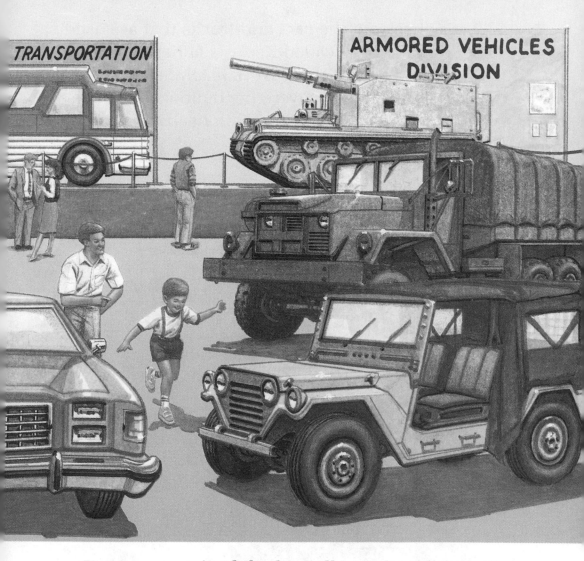

Kenny recognized the big yellow school bus and the modern city bus. There was even a double-decker bus, and a yellow taxi. But Kenny was most interested in the green and brown vehicles.

"The jeep, the tank, and the canvas-covered truck are all used by the army to transport soldiers," explained his father. Kenny ran off to sit in the jeep.

"Let's check out the cars and trucks that are used to build our roads," called Kenny's father.

Kenny had a lot of these work machines in his toy collection. His favorites were the bulldozer and the ditchdigger, which rip up roads in need of repair.

There was also a dump truck, a cement mixer, and an asphalt spreader, which are used to make new roads when the old ones are torn up.

"Watching the cement mixer go round and round can sure make you dizzy," said Kenny.

Kenny didn't know where to look first in the delivery car and truck area. He saw the big freezer truck, which he had in his toy collection at home. But Kenny also loved the long fuel oil tanker and the mail delivery van.

"I have that truck at home, too," exclaimed Kenny as he pointed to a long flat truck used for carrying new cars to the dealers. "I can pile eight of my little cars on it."

At the mobile home area Kenny asked, "Dad, does our house have wheels hidden underneath it? We could take it for a ride sometime!"

"No, I'm afraid not," his father answered with a chuckle. "These trailers are special houses that are designed to be on the move. All of the furniture is nailed down so nothing falls when the home is on the road."

The repair truck and van area was one of the show's most popular places. "The cherry picker is used when broken lights or telephone wires need repair. We stand on the platform and the crane lifts us all the way up to the problem area," explained the service person.

As Kenny rode up high in the cherry picker, he saw some of the other repair vehicles. "There's a tow truck for broken cars," said Kenny.

"That's right," said his father. "And that van carries different tools to help fix plumbing systems, or broken boilers, or anything else in need of repair."

Kenny and his father stopped for ice cream before they moved on to the next area.

"I'm having a great time," said Kenny. "And we haven't even gotten to the race cars yet!"

"Well, let's go," said his father.

On the way they had to pass through the service truck area.

"There's the sanitation truck, which picks up garbage, and the snowplow, which clears the roads after a snowstorm, and the street cleaner, which sprays water," Kenny said.

When Kenny looked into the next area, he jumped with excitement.

"Come on," he shouted. "It's the racing cars!"

There were red cars and white cars and blue cars and cars with pinstripes on them. And they could all go very, very fast.

"Can I try on your helmet?" Kenny asked the man at the booth.

"You can have your own helmet," the man said, handing Kenny a shiny blue-and-white sample. "You can even sit behind the wheel," he added as he placed Kenny in the driver's seat.

"Vroom, vroom!" said Kenny.

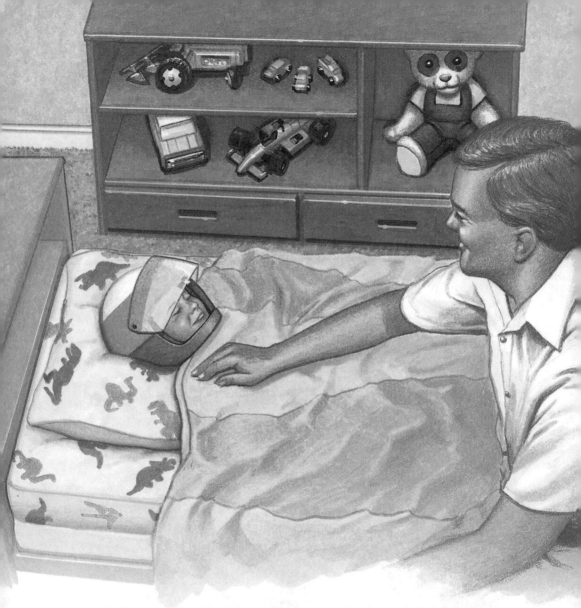

"That was the best day ever," Kenny told his father that night at bedtime. "I learned so much about different cars and trucks, and I love my new helmet!"

"I can see," said Kenny's father, laughing.